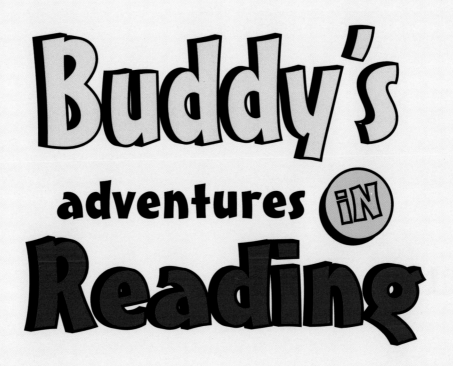

Buddy's adventures in Reading

John Whyte

VANTAGE PRESS
New York

Published by Vantage Press, Inc.
419 Park Ave. South, New York, NY 10016

Manufactured in the United States of America
ISBN: 0-533-15641-6

Library of Congress Catalog Card No.: 2006908674

0 9 8 7 6 5 4 3 2 1

In a land far away
where dragons can **FLY**

"Where are my wings?"
poor Buddy did **CRY**.

First learn to read
then you can FLY.

Words give you wings
to reach the SKY.

Then Father said,
"To read, you must **SEEK**

the hairy people on

the mountain **PEAK**."

Climb, Buddy climbed towards the white TOP

But he could not read **STOP**

Down Buddy fell
happy to FLOAT

On the ocean blue
aboard a big BOAT.

West Buddy sailed with
Pirate Shark CREW

Then landed on sand

"Now what should I **DO**?"

But Buddy wants words
and wings are not **SOLD**!

So glum Buddy walked through the forest on FEET.

No word, no wings,
no Hairy People to MEET.

When up in a tree,

in the bright SUN

Two little creatures

reading for **FUN**.

"My name is Buddy, how do you DO?"

"We're the Hairy People,
                    pleased to meet YOU."

"Hurray!" shouted Buddy,
                    "Just the friends I NEED

I must get my wings,
                    please teach me to READ."

"Take the big blue book
from the **BOUGH**

It's magic, it speaks and
teaches you **HOW**.

Read you will but first
you must START

To see a word as
more than one PART.

The mountain you climbed
is easy to **SAY**

But to learn how to read
this is the **WAY**."

Moun --- Tain

Try, Buddy tried
and tried all **DAY**

Then all of a sudden
he said "HURRAY!"

"The parts of the word
have become ONE

I can read mountain
so now I am **DONE**."

"Thanks," Buddy waved

to his friends in the TREE

And turned to the ocean
and what did he **SEE**?

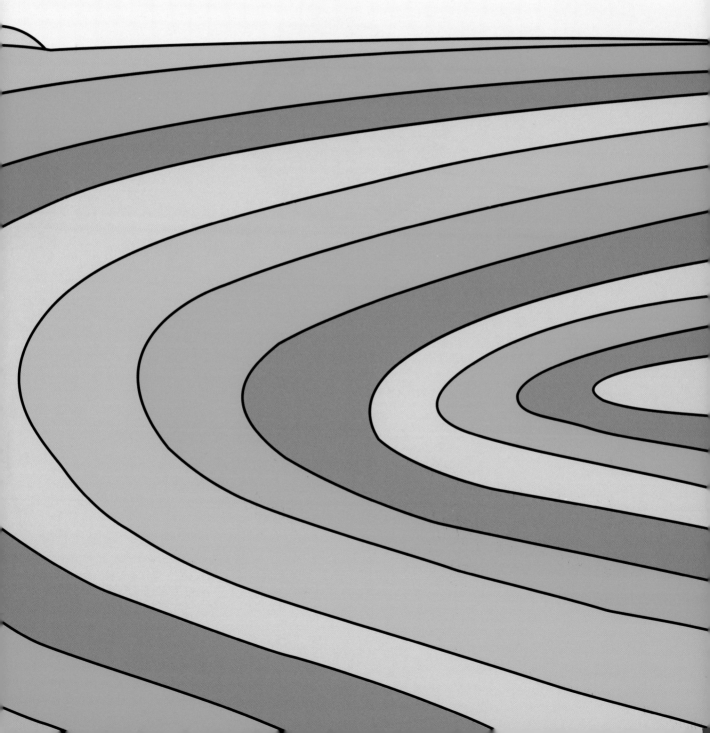

About the Author

Toronto-born, Vancouver-based illustrator John Whyte has drawn from his experience as someone with life-long learning disabilities to create an engaging and educational book for children called Buddy's Adventures in Reading. The story focuses on Buddy, a little dragon that has to learn to read in order to earn his wings and fly.

Buddy's story mirrors many of John's struggles with reading and self-esteem. John is dyslexic and at the age of 42 he can't spell simple words and struggles to fill out a job application.

John's childhood was what psychologists might call troubled or dysfunctional. But for John, it was simply a confusing and frightening time that saw him moved from inner city school to inner city school, essentially lost in the endless shuffle and never properly diagnosed as having a learning disability. As a result, he had few friends and suffered outright bullying, a situation aggravated by his apparent 'slowness' due to dyslexia. They were hard times that stripped John of his self-confidence and left him feeling worthless and unwanted.

Life became difficult to the point that John found himself living on the street just trying to survive bleak day after bleak day with a future that at times seemed impossible. The one thing John had, the only thing in a world that had forgotten about him, and the one thing he could do much better than most was draw.

So he did and an early doodle on the back of a napkin caught the eye of another customer in a downtown diner. The stranger offered to pay John $1 for the drawing. It was a modest start to growing confidence in the fact he had a special talent.

With the $1 he bought a bigger drawing pad and drew for people who passed by him on the street. They loved his work and instilled John with a sense of worth: he could make people happy. There was little monetary reward but he got a couple of bucks here and there and bought successively bigger drawing pads.

 After several years of sleeping in parks or on hot air vents, John managed to get a job on a construction site as a labourer—a job he would hold for the next 25 years. Through the haze of concrete dust, it was always clear to him that drawing would be his escape from the daily drudgery of carrying bricks and being shut out of the literate world.

At the age of 19, tired of feeling ostracized and ashamed of his illiteracy, John decided he would teach himself to read. He went to his father for advice on how to begin and his father said: if you want to learn how to read, whenever you walk past a sign look at the words and break them down into smaller parts. John did a lot of walking and eventually managed to read a lot of the signs he passed.

In 2005, John hit on the idea of creating a book to help small children avoid the problems he had had with spelling and reading and consequently the negative impact these difficulties had imposed on his life. It was an inspired, magical idea, that resulted in the loveable little Buddy the dragon—a character sure to be a favourite with children and parents alike.

Plans are underway for two follow-up books. Who knows what John and Buddy will get up to next?

Kudos

This book would not be possible without the help of the following people.

John Callander taught at the Manitoba Theatre for Young People. His Children's play Cinderfella was produced at the Prairie Theatre Exchange, Winnipeg. John currently lives in Vancouver where he works as a writer and actor. He was recently nominated for two Leo awards - Best Screenwriter and Best Supporting Male Actor. Winner - Best Screenplay

Kevin Plain is a writer and editor living in Vancouver, British Columbia. He has a Master of Arts degree in English from Simon Fraser University.

Reva Diana is a graphic and web designer, developer, illustrator and all around geekette. She currently lives in Vancouver with two mischievous monkeys – Ava and Arys.

And a big thank you to Mike Rosengarten, a pre-press and print technician living in Vancouver, with inspiration from his son, Kyle.